The ADVENTURES of UNCLE STINKY

BOOK 1

THE GOOD, THE BAD, AND THE SMELLY

BY CHRIS RUMBLE

TRICYCLE PRESS
Berkeley/Toronto

WARNING

The contents of this book are extremely stinky and may not be suitable for some readers.

READER DISCRETION ADVISED.

Ridiculously Enormous Thanks

To Cathy, my beautiful wife: I love having you as a partner in a life that is truly a wonderful adventure. To Zachary and Kara: You two are the greatest sidekicks a dad ever had. To Mom and Dad: who taught me unconditional love, uncontained laughter, and to march to the beat of a different drummer. To my brothers, Matthew, Michael, and Butch: inspiring difference makers all. To Cheryl: my cheerleader, my sister, my friend. To Kara, again, for her work on Lester and to David for his presidential research. To every teacher and principal and librarian who allowed me the joy of reading and singing with their students: Thanks, especially, to Mrs. Ingle and her second grade class of 2001–2002 for loving Uncle Stinky. To Nicole: who pulled Uncle Stinky out of the slush pile. To God: who pulled *me* out of the slush pile.

Tricycle Press
a little division of Ten Speed Press
P.O. Box 7123
Berkeley, California 94707
www.tenspeed.com

Design by Betsy Stromberg
Typeset in Bailey Quad, Bailey Sans, Oxtail, Shannon, Stone Sans, and Stone Serif
The illustrations in this book were rendered in pen and ink.

Library of Congress Cataloging-in-Publication Data

Rumble, Chris, 1961-
  The good, the bad, and the smelly / by Chris Rumble.
    p. cm. -- (The adventures of Uncle Stinky)
Summary: Appropriately named Uncle Stinky, his pickle sidekick, and his two nephews save the town of Hootenholler from a really big blue dog and a plague of embarrassment.
  ISBN 1-58246-120-1
  [1. Adventure and adventurers--Fiction. 2. Humorous stories.] I. Title.
PZ7.R88765 Go 2004
[Fic]--dc22
                              2003018265
Hardcover ISBN 1-58246-120-1
Paperback ISBN 1-58246-122-8
First Tricycle Press printing, 2004
Printed in Canada
1 2 3 4 5 6 — 08 07 06 05 04

CONTENTS

PLEASE NOTE: Some settling of contents
normally occurs during shipping and handling.

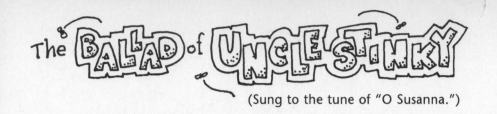

The BALLAD of UNCLE STINKY

(Sung to the tune of "O Susanna.")

1. Now Uncle Stinky goes around doin' deeds of love,

You'd think the man was sent to Earth straight from heav'n above!

He scares off all the bad dudes, but wouldn't hurt a mouse,

He's great to have around your town...just not in your house!

CHORUS:
Uncle Stinky,
Best friend I ever had!
I never met a man so good
Who smelled so awful bad!

2. When ol' Stinky was a boy, his folks, they loved him so,

Sent him off to school each day, a-smilin' as he'd go!

Teacher knew this special boy was different from them all,

Gave to him a special desk... in a room way down the hall!

(Sing the CHORUS here. C'mon! LOUDER!)

4

3. If you ever get a chance to know him like I do,

You'd find that you would love the man,
and he would love you, too!

When you cross ol' Stinky's path, this is all I wish:

Please ignore the way he smells...like onions and old fish!

(Sing the CHORUS again. This time add Broadway dance moves!)

(Sing it again...OPERA STYLE!)

(Sing it again and again and again. See how many times you can sing it before someone begs you to stop!)

sniff
sniff

HOW UNCLE STINKY GOT HIS SIDEKICKS

Episode 1

My name is Zack, and this is my little brother Billy. We have an uncle named "Stinky." If he has another name, we've never heard it. I wish I could tell you that I don't know how he got his name, but I do know. He smells like old fish and onions.

Hehwo.

All of the folks in the town of Hootenholler agree on this point. Not that the city council took an official survey or anything. But the minute someone gets a snort of Stinky's stink, they agree. "Whew, boy. That says it all right. Onions and old fish."

A day in the life of Uncle Stinky...

Uncle Stinky has a sidekick. A sidekick is a loyal friend who always shares your adventures. A great sidekick stands with you even when you're facing the most ferocious villains.

Uncle Stinky's sidekick is named "Pickle." I know how he got *his* name, too. He *is* a pickle! That's right… an actual pickle. Uncle Stinky can tell you all about it.

"Oh, I gave them regular sidekicks a shot. You know, the run-of-the-mill sidekicks that the regular adventurers always have. I tried the little short sidekick who talks kind of funny, always does what you say, and has a name like Igor or Boo-Boo. I tried the brainiac sidekick. You know the kind. They can't judo chop or swing from a chandelier worth a hoot, but they can do all sorts of calculations without any help from their teachers. I even tried the dog sidekick! Those dog sidekicks are amazin'! They're smarter than human beings, yet they still don't get any real respect.

I think dogs never get any real respect because they're always sniffin' everything. You know what I mean? Dogs and people who are always sniffin' stuff are never thought of very highly, no matter how smart they are.

"Think about it. No one known for going around sniffin' stuff all the time has ever been elected president.

Name of President	A Sniffer	NOT a Sniffer	Additional Notes
George Washington		✓	Only sniffed a couple of cherries as a boy.
John Adams		✓	No way
Thomas Jefferson		✓	Declared his independence from sniffing early on.
James Madison		✓	Not even one of Dolly's cupcakes
James Monroe		✓	Only unfounded rumors
John Quincy Adams		✓	Followed in his father's non-sniffing footsteps.
Andrew Jackson		✓	"Old Hickory"—are you kidding?
Martin Van Buren		✓	Even his wife said she never saw him sniffing anything.
William Henry Harrison		✓	Pneumonia left him too weak to sniff.
John Tyler		✓	Completely anti-sniffing
James K. Polk		✓	You'd think a guy named "Polk" would sniff stuff, but he didn't.
Zachary Taylor		✓	Totally sniff free
Millard Fillmore		✓	Rumored to be a closet sniffer, but was never caught.
Franklin Pierce		✓	Get outta here!
James Buchanan		✓	Was known to inhale quite vigorously but not enough to qualify as sniffing
Abraham Lincoln		✓	Three score years with no sniffing
Andrew Johnson		✓	He was impeached, but sniffing not the issue.

Ulysses S. Grant		✓	The "S" stood for "Simpson," not "Sniffer."
Rutherford B. Hayes		✓	Highly suspected but never convicted
James Garfield		✓	Enjoyed the aroma of coffee but never caught blatantly sniffing.
Chester Arthur		✓	Postnasal drip sometimes mistaken for sniffing.
Grover Cleveland		✓	Some still swear he sniffed things every night while everyone else slept.
Benjamin Harrison		✓	If he sniffed, he was very sneaky about it.
William McKinley		✓	Confessed to being greatly tempted, but never gave in.
Theodore Roosevelt		✓	Walked softly. Carried a big stick. Never sniffed.
William Howard Taft		✓	Sinuses too congested to make sniffing even a possibility.
Woodrow Wilson		✓	Lobbied for anti-sniffing clause in League of Nations Charter.
Warren G. Harding		✓	Some claim they heard sniffing noises behind the Oval Office door.
Calvin Coolidge		✓	Nope. Called "Silent Cal" for a reason.
Herbert Hoover		✓	Enjoyed sniffing flowers, but who cares?
Franklin D. Roosevelt		✓	Sniffing would have dashed all hopes of being elected four times.
Harry S. Truman		✓	Signed proclamation renouncing sniffing.
Dwight D. Eisenhower		✓	NOT THIS GENERAL!
John F. Kennedy		✓	If he had, people would have looked the other way due to popularity.
Lyndon B. Johnson		✓	Once he started to sniff his ink pen, but caught himself.
Richard M. Nixon		✓	After his resignation, he sniffed like there was no tomorrow.
Gerald R. Ford		✓	Fell down a lot, but did not sniff.
Jimmy Carter		✓	Sniffed peanuts only, but public understood.
Ronald Reagan		✓	He wouldn't sniff anything, not even for "the Gipper."
George H. W. Bush		✓	Read my lips…NO SNIFFING!
Bill Clinton		✓	Depends on what your definition of "sniff" is.
George W. Bush		✓	While at his ranch, sniffed something on his shoe, but he was on vacation.

"Not one true sniffer in the bunch!"

Anyway, Uncle Stinky tried ordinary sidekicks, but they couldn't stand to be around him long enough to finish out an entire adventure. Most of the time, the adventure never even had a chance to get started!

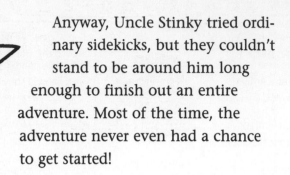

"That's right, little buddy. It's the strangest thing…those little boogers would run away before the villain even did anything wrong! I couldn't figger it out for the life of me! While ol' Dr. Frankenstein was still readin' the directions on how to put his spooky monster together, my sidekick would skedaddle!

"My sidekick would already be running for home while the Wicked Witch of the West was still just a young'un in kindygarden.

"Or, my sidekick would head for the hills while the Godziller monster was still just an egg."

So when the tales of Uncle Stinky and his sidekicks were told, they were not very interesting at all. They would go something like this:

"Uncle Stinky and his sidekick Goober walked down the street a little ways and then Goober couldn't hold his breath any longer so he ran away. The end."

I think you would agree: That is not a very exciting story. It certainly could never be made into a movie. Movies have to be at least long enough to eat a box of gummy bears.

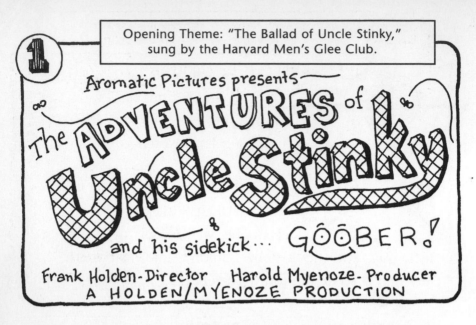

1 Opening Theme: "The Ballad of Uncle Stinky," sung by the Harvard Men's Glee Club.

2 Birds singing. Music: light, airy arrangement of "The Ballad of Uncle Stinky."

18

Stinky has lost his share of sidekicks, but he's just tickled pink with Pickle. He loves to brag about his little green buddy....

"Pickle has lots of sidekickin' talents. I let a few other inanimate objects try out for the job, but found Pickle to be the best!

"For example, if we're doin' spy work in a dangerous place, we often have to do what's called 'layin' low.' That's where you have to be real still and quiet 'til the bad guy leaves the room. You won't find a sidekick better at layin' low than Pickle.

"Sometimes our adventures require us to slip into places without bein' noticed. We adventurers call this 'goin' undercover.' Pickle has made me as proud as a peacock with his undercover work. Last Thanksgivin', he was smack dab in the middle o' the 'Booger Hill' Gang's celebration. There he was, hidin' in the horn o' plenty! He heard all o' their plans to rob Belinda's Baloney Boutique, and they never even knew he was there!

"More than anything else, sidekicks have to be able to keep a secret. No matter what the meanies do to him, all o' my adventurer secrets are safe with Pickle!"

Stinky loves Pickle, but he knows Pickle is not perfect. He knows he's not exactly the greatest sidekick when it comes to things like cracking secret codes...

jumping canyons…

and bodyslamming bad guys.

But at least he stays with Stinky throughout an entire adventure. As Stinky said to me just this morning, "I never had a sidekick more loyal than good ol' Pickle. He is true blue…or green…or whatever. The point is, he's always there for me, no matter what."

When he said that, I got a lump in my throat. Not the kind you get when you swallow a rock or an acorn or something.

The kind you get when you are about to cry.

No one should face the villains of this world alone. I know Uncle Stinky would make the best of a bad situation. He always does. But he deserves better company than a kosher dill.

So, after giving it some thought, I figured Uncle Stinky could use some *real sidekicks*—and we could use some real adventure!

26

TOGETHER we'll do our best to rid the world of other horrors, like school lunches.

TOGETHER we'll learn to face trouble head on and come out smiling on the other side!

We'll never be without one another, never apart, always together,

the FOUR of us: Uncle Stinky, Billy, me...

...and MY CLOTHESPIN!

As for Pickle... Uncle Stinky hooked him up with the Dill County Police Department where he solves crimes with Detective Gherkin.
He relishes every day.
But he still goes undercover and stays close to Uncle Stinky. He shows up six more times in the rest of the book.
Can you spot him?

(answers on page 95)

PIONEER UNIVERSITY

with ZACK and BILLY

Since we're going to be adventurers, Billy and I decided to start an adventurer's school for kids. We call it Pioneer University. You'll learn important stuff every time you come to P.U.

TODAY'S LESSON: How To Wear a CLOTHESPIN!

(You're gonna need this if you're gonna join our adventures!)

First, you gotta figure out what kind of nose you got.

Some noses fall into three additional categories, not by how they look, but for what's coming out of 'em.

NOSE I.D. CHART
Pick your nose:

 Bulb
 Skeeter-Bite
Needle

 Hook
 Ski-Slope
 Oinker
 Potato

PICK WHAT'S COMIN' OUT OF 'EM!

 Hanging Gardens
 Inchworm Races
 BOOGER-RAMA!

If your nose falls into one of these categories, you're gonna have to get rid of what's in 'em before a clothespin will work. Wipe...pluck...blow...whack... dig...vacuum...dynamite... whatever it takes.

31

All clear? Good! Now, take our Nose Identification Chart to the mirror and figure out which catagory your nose falls into. This is important because this will determine what kind of clothespin you need. A clothespin that doesn't fit right can leave you in just as much danger as a kid without a clothespin.

Once you've identified your nose type, use the sizing chart to find out what kind of clothespin we recommend and where to get it.

When you get your clothespin, it'll pinch your nose a little at first, but don't worry, you'll get used to it. Go ahead, clamp that bad boy shut, and you'll be READY FOR ADVENTURE!

OFFICIAL CLOTHESPIN SIZING CHART RU

NOSE TYPE	THE CLOTHESPIN YOU NEED	WHERE TO GET IT
Bulb	Clampett's, #4	Wendell's Eggs-N-Things Things Department
Hook	High and Dry, Size B	"The SoapOpera" All Nite Laundromat and Bingo Parlor (in the vending machine)
Ski-Slope	U-Pin-Em, Model XGT	Big Honkin' Mart o' Plenty Housewares, Aisle 37
Skeeter-Bite	The one in the "I Love Laundry" Fantasy Play Set	Big Honkin' Mart O' Plenty Toy Department, Aisle 89
Needle	Anti-Stink Device	Stan's Stand (Stan invented it himself) Ask for it by name
Oinker	Clampett's, #2	"Eat Here and Get Gas" Gas Station, Grill and Quick Mart (next to the Beef Jerky)
Potato	"Iron Man" Extra Large Vise Grip (very rare)	Hootenholler Industrial Fasteners Warehouse (go to the back door, ask for "Big Head")

The Asteamed Pioneer University Fackulty:
ZACK- Perfesser #1   BILLY- Perfesser #2
" Teaching kids IMPORTANT STUFF since 2004."

ZACK AND BILLY ANSWER YOUR QUESTIONS

Now it's time to open up the PU mailbag! Billy, why don't you read the first question?

Q: What's up, Zack and Billy? Can my nose fall into more than one category?

A: *Oh, sure! It's called a combo. We see them on occasion and we have special charts for them. In fact, just yesterday, we saw a "needle-hook" and an "oinker-skeeter bite."*

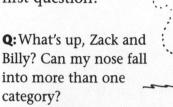

Needle-Hook   Oinker-Skeeter-Bite

It took some skill, but we were able to fit them and send 'em off happy. It's all in the diagnosis.

Q: Zack and Billy, I'm a little worried. How can I tell if my clothespin is really going to protect me?

A: *If you can blow air out your nose, it ain't gonna work! Stink has a way finding its way through the smallest secret passage left by an improperly fitting clothespin. As we always say here at PU: "If air can get out, stink'll get in."*

Q: What if I have done everything just the way you said and I'm still getting stink?

A: *You probably put your nose in the wrong category. Some people just don't want to admit what kinda nose they got. Their pride puts them in harm's way. A few weeks ago we tried to help a lady who kept sayin' she had a "needle," when even Billy could plainly see she had a very rare "bulb-hook-potato" triple combo. To this day she refuses to admit what kind of nose she has, even though she has to endure a lotta stink.*

Bulb·Hook·
Potato

Q: Hey, Zack, how come Billy never wears a clothespin when he's on an adventure with Uncle Stinky?

A: *That's a good question, my friend. Let's see, how can I explain Billy? I can answer best like this:* He just does not care! *In fact, he seems to* enjoy the smell!

Zack and BILLY

36

HEY, KIDS... I KNOW YER EXCITED AND ALL, BUT YA DON'T HAVE TO SCREAM "YAY" AT EVERYTHING I SAY.

"Listen up now, kids, cause ya won't hear my stories any-where else in the whole wide world! I made 'em up all by myself. They just popped outta my own little brain. Little Billy draws all the pictures. He's not just an artist...he's an arTEEST—a regular Michael Angeloo. He even wrote the words! (I had to help with the spellin' though.)

Yay.

"The title of today's story is *Buford, the Ridiculously Enormous Blue Dog!*"

Let's get closer...

Shush, Wayne! I cain't hear!

BUFORD the ridikulusly enormus Blue Dog

BY UNKEC STINKEE

Pikchurs by Little BILLY

37

DEDICATION

I'd like to send out a big honkin' YEEEEEE-HAW to: Mommy and Daddy: who love me no matter what, stink and all. Zack and Billy: the greatest nephews and sidekicks an adventurer ever had. You could never know how much you little dudes mean to me. K.C.: my brave and beautiful niece, who lives life to the fullest and never wears a clothespin around me. Pickle: I'll never forget you, and I'll never eat another pickle as long as I live. Mrs. Hooper: my fifth grade teacher who taught me all about writin' English good. All the wonderful kids who love listenin' to my stories as much as I love readin' 'em!

BUFORD

the ridikulusly enormus Blue Dog

BY UNKEL STINKEE   PiKCHURS BY Little BILLY

One day the neighborhood dogs, Chloe, Chicken-Bone, and Max, decided to play a game of Red Rover.

the Nayborhud DOGS

KLOEE   CHICKIN BONE   MAX

Buford, the new dog on the block, heard 'em gettin' up the game and he came a-runnin', sayin', "I wanna play! I wanna play!"

As Buford came boundin' toward the other dogs, the ground shook so much and such shock and terror went through their little doggie bodies that Chicken-Bone wet himself.

You gotta understand, kids, Buford is *huge*. He's BIGGER 'N A HOUSE. And on top of that, he's BLUE! Can you imagine what could happen to the town of Hootenholler if he decided to go lookin' for buried bones?

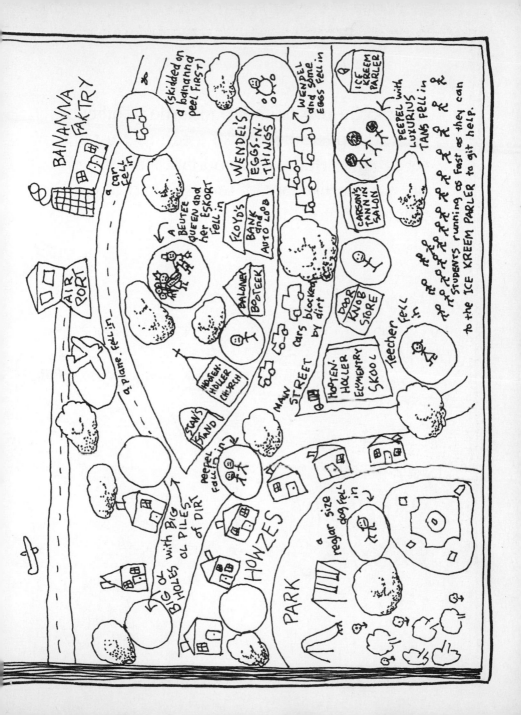

His diggin' could compromise the stability of the rocky plates beneath the earth's crust and set off an earthquake. Important elements of our society, like tannin' salons, could careen helplessly into a deep, undulatin' crevasse.

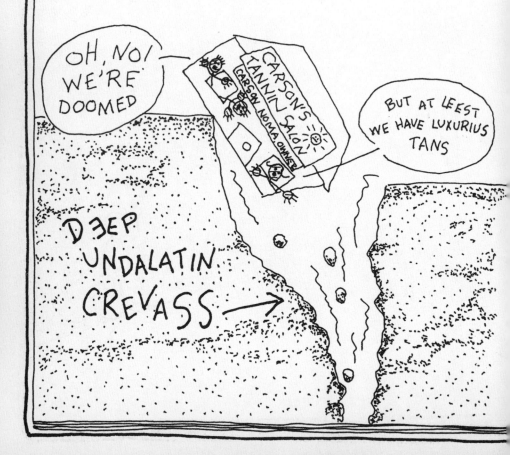

And, where's a dog this big gonna git enough food to be properly nourished? Guard your crops, farmers! And remember, dogs are carnivores, too. That means they eat meat! So do whatever it takes to protect yer cattle, 'cause here comes Buford! And he's *hongry!*

And what about *after* he eats? C'mon, kids, you all are smart enough to know what I'm gettin' at! Who's gonna clean up after this pooch, yer momma? I don't think so! It would take a steam shovel and a few good hours of hard labor to finish that job!

Anyway, before they had a chance to really think through this situation, Chicken-Bone said, "Well...uh...sure...I guess you can play."

Buford said, "I'll be one team, and you guys can be the other team!"

"Okay."

"You all can call Red Rover first."

"Red Rover! Red Rover! Send...uh...um..."

"Buford! My name is Buford."

LIKE I ALLWAYS SAY...
THE MORE THE MERRIER

"Red Rover! Red Rover!
Send...BUFORD right over!"

Buford came a-racin' across the field.
He picked up a big head of steam.

The other dogs gripped each other's paws
tightly and closed their eyes.

What happened next would be funny had it not been so unpleasant for one of them little puppies.

Basically what happened was…um…uh… well…ya see…

Chicken-Bone got squashed is what happened.

Yes sir, he was purty flat, indeed. Just then, outta nowhere came this big ol' team of doctors and nurses, and they went to tryin' to fluff him up again.

Buford, although ludicrously large, is not a mean sort o' pooch at all. In fact, he felt just awful about what happened.

He figgered the least he could do was to give 'em a hand...or a paw, or whatever...so he ran in the general direction of the doctors and nurses and tried to get up close so's he could be real helpful and all.

When he did that...well, ya see...uh...
the thing is...um...

Buford sort o' squashed that team of doctors and nurses is what happened.

When they heard that Chicken-Bone was flatter 'n a pancake, the people in the town were a bit perturbed. They got more upset when they heard that the good-hearted doctors and nurses were squished like cock-a-roaches. But when they heard what could possibly happen to their tannin' salons... they were downright furious! They wanted somethin' done about Buford.

Just then, a familiar prehistoric creature named Barnaby and his little friend Boppy Babe came into town. They marched down the street dancin' and singin', all happy and sweet, but between you an' me, it was kinda irritatin'.

They told the angry townspeople that everybody just needed to hug each other. Then they taught 'em a song called, "Friends Who Are Friendly Have Friends Who Are Friendly Friends." So there they were, all bunched up together, huggin' and a-smilin' and a-singin'.

Now Buford, although monstrously massive, is a tenderhearted critter. In fact, he began to feel all giggly inside. He saw everybody huggin' and a-smilin' and a-singin', and he wanted to be a part of the celebration! So he skipped happily over to the friendly friends.

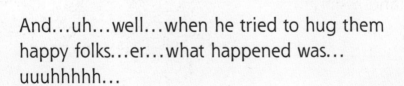

And...uh...well...when he tried to hug them happy folks...er...what happened was... uuuhhhhh...

Buford squashed Barnaby, Boppy Babe, and all them Friendly Friends is what happened.

I could go on with the rest of the story, but I'm afraid it's just too much mayhem and carnage for you young'uns to stomach. I don't want any of my little buddies to go havin' any nightmares about Buford.

The most important thing
is that we all learn somethin', right? So, here's
what we learn from
this tragic tale:

LESSON #1: If you're gettin' up
a playground game like "Dodge
Ball" or "Duck-Duck-Goose" or "Spank the
Possum" or whatever, and along comes a dog who
ain't dog colored, start gatherin' up your belongin's.

LESSON #2: If that strange-colored dog is bigger 'n a
dump truck, RUN LIKE THE DICKENS!

GULP!

And, kids, there are many more songs that will bring you just as much entertainment! Tunes like...

"Hap-Hap-Hap-Hap-Hap-Hap-Hap-Hap-Hap-Hap-Hap-Happy Boy"

"It's Not Nice to Pluck Daddy's Nose Hairs while He's Taking a Nap"

"Hello, Mellow Fellow, Would You Like Some Jell-O?"

"Safe Kids Wear Goggles (When Using the Chain Saw)"

"If You're Gassy and You Know It, Go Outside"

"Internal Organ ABCs"

"Good Morning, Mr. Sunshine (Please Don't Hurt Me with Your Dangerous Ultraviolet Rays)"

"Let's All Ride on the Potty Train"

Plus, as a special BONUS, Boppy Babe's solo "I Love You Bunches Even Though You're Odd."

You can have all these songs on one CD or cassette for only $99.95! Call 555-FUNHAPPYTASTIC today!

5 buckaroos

WHAT THEY'RE SAYING ABOUT BUFORD...

"Every home and school should have multiple copies of *Buford, the Ridiculously Enormous Blue Dog*. Not only is it a literary classic, it is also a wonderful tool for educating our precious pupils to be consciously aware of the dangers of playing field games with curiously colored canines of preposterous proportions."
—Dr. Deloris Tenchen, *principal, Hootenholler Elementary*

"Buford's awesome, but he needs a sidekick. I'm available."
—Goober, *unemployed sidekick*

"In Buford Uncle Stinky has developed a character so real I felt like the events of the story were happening to me. I cheered as I considered the damage Buford could inflict on a small town. Tears streaked down my cheeks as I felt along with him the intolerance of the ignorant townspeople."
—Godziller, *gargantuan fire-breathing lizard*

"Dang! That dawg's bigger 'n one o' my blue ribbon hawgs."
—Pop Widener, *host of "Pop Widener's Hogs on Parade"*

"That Buford sure can create a lotta carnage and mayhem. We like the squashin' parts."
—The Booger Hill Gang: Randolf, Martin, and Wayne, *notorious food bandits*

ISBN 6-2731-711-02

UNCLE STINKY saves HOOTENHOLLER from the DREADFUL PLAGUE of EMBARRASSMENT

Episode 2

As you have figured out by now, Uncle Stinky is a kind of superhero because he's always looking for ways to help others. He can't stand to just sit back and watch someone else go through tough times alone. I've heard the folks of Hootenholler say it at least a gazillion times: "Ol' Stinky's got a heart of gold..." then they always add, "...and he stinks to high heaven."

SUPAH HEEWO?

67

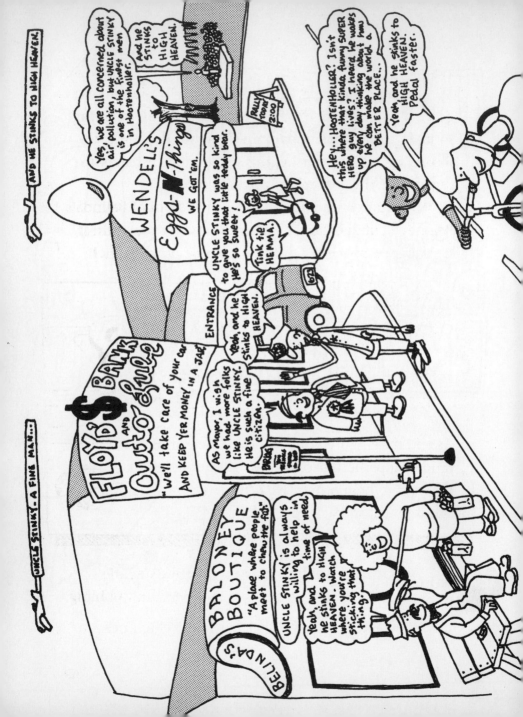

Yesterday morning, Stinky, Billy, and I were walking down Huppupenna Way, and I said, "How are we going to make a difference today, Unk?" About that time, we looked up and saw Mrs. Ginnysquat's dog Lester zooming around the corner, chasing a squirrel.

The squirrel ran under the bench in front of Belinda's Baloney Boutique. Lester was so focused on the squirrel, he slammed his head right into the side of that bench.

Lester kind of wobbled down the sidewalk a little ways. Then he looked up and saw us *seeing* him wobbling. Uncle Stinky tells this part better than I do.

"It was heart-breakin', wasn't it, Zack? The poor doggie already has to deal with havin' to wear a Weenie Wheelie 3000 to keep his gut from draggin'! When ol' Lester realized we'd seen him smack into that bench, I think he was blushin' under his fur.

"Then the pitiful puppy tried to hide behind the No Parkin' sign, and it hit me!

"We had our quest for the day! We were goin' to do everything in our power to make sure no one in Hootenholler suffered from the dreadful plague of embarrassment!

"And I *do* know a little bit about the pain and agony of being

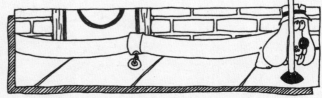

embarrassed. Remember the time Ramona Rippinsnort was about go on stage at the Hootenholler Beauty Contest? Ramona's famous for her big, beau-tiful head o' *natcherly* curly hair. Well, sir, she was all dolled up and lookin' extry purty that night.

NO PARKING
YOU
TEENAGERS
SHOULD
know better.

"I went to wish her luck, and my stink straightened her trademark hairdo. Now THAT was embarrassin'.

"And then there was the time the Hootenholler City Council gave everyone in town gas masks. Everyone, that is, except me! It was humiliatin' to say the least.

"After 'while, Samuel Naise came struttin' down Huppupenna Way. Suddenly, a big gust o' wind kicked up, blowin' leaves, Lester, and Samuel's comb-over ever' which-a-way.

"Now, before we can go on, you young'uns need to know what a comb-over is. When some men go bald, they fool everybody into thinkin' they have a full head o' hair by growin' out the two or three hairs they do have real long and combin' 'em *over*. They "comb-over" their hairs so's nobody knows they are bald as a cantaloupe. It's pure genius.

"Comb-overs are kinda like snowflakes: No two are alike. Some take years to cultivate and are veritable works o' art.

"From where we were standin' we could see a large group of people coming down Warjalurnta Drive and they would soon cross paths with Mr. Naise. We knew we had to do something quick!

"Now, Samuel Naise is the mayor of Hootenholler. That's right, he's Mayor Naise. And there he was standin' in the middle of town with all of his baldness reflecting the midday sun, and registered voters comin' down the street! They were on a collision course! You can see how this could be embarrassin' and possibly even damagin' to his political career.

"I knew I had to act quickly. I always carry a clump o' worms in my vest pocket 'cause ya never know when yer gonna come across a fishin' hole. But, there are a lot more uses for worms than just catchin' fish! I pulled out three o' them worms and held 'em up for my flies.

"Each fly took a worm and knew exactly what to do! Flyin' in formation, they crossed the street, hovered over Mayor Naise for a split second, and then dropped their worms with great precision on his head, arrangin' them to look exactly like his comb-over.

The X FLIES

TOP SECRET!

HUH?

BIG AM FAHUU

THE POOP is OUT THERE.

MISSION #4537: OPERATION COMB-OVER

"My flies were already back across the street and swarmin' around me as usual when the crowd crossed paths with Mayor Naise…

"Whew! We pulled it off! Not one of those voters noticed the difference between the mayor's comb-over and the worms! Mission accomplished!"

Mizzen accompwish!

SLAP!

Hey, Unk, what happened next is worth mentioning, too. I guess it was lunchtime for the birds on Huppupenna Way, because about nine of them landed on the mayor's head and began to enjoy the worms. They didn't just grab the worms and leave. No, they gathered up there like a family sitting down to Thanksgiving dinner.

As the mayor passed another group of voters he just smiled and waved and, being the quick thinker that he is, broke into song…

The voters stared in amazement at their mayor. They wondered how he could be so kind and gentle that little birdies would come to rest on his head. They had never seen a man who was in such harmony with nature!

77

"That's right, little buddy! The folks of this town saw somethin' that day they will never forget…but they *didn't* see the mayor's bald head. And, at least for a little while, the town of Hootenholler was saved from the dreadful plague of embarrassment!

"Theo Durzindapance saw the whole thing. He came up and started slappin' me on the back, sayin', 'Great job, Stinky! Great job!' I had to tell him to stop 'cause just knowin' no one was embarrassed was enough for me. He finally did stop his silly back slappin', but I noticed he sorta follered us around for the rest of the day, admirin' my good deeds."

A few minutes later, a van loaded with apples stopped in front of Stan's Stand. Along with it came our next assignment. Take it away, Unk!

78

"Now Stan usually stands in front of his stand and sells fruits and vegetables. Stan stands in front of his stand all day, or at least as long as he can stand it. Stan's wife's name is Charity, but we all call her "Chare" for short. Charity sits in the rear of the store. Which is kinda interestin' when ya think about it: Stan stands while Chare sits. Anyway, you can ponder that later...

"Stan's son, Van, natcherly, drives the van. This was one huge vanload of apples, and there wasn't much room for 'em on Stan's stand. So Stan told Van to park the van in the rear of Stan's Stand next to Chare's chair. He told Van that he would just send anybody wantin' apples 'round back, and Chare could take care of their apple-buyin' needs. In fact, he said, he would just make a sign so everybody'd know where to git apples...
...and that's exactly what he did."

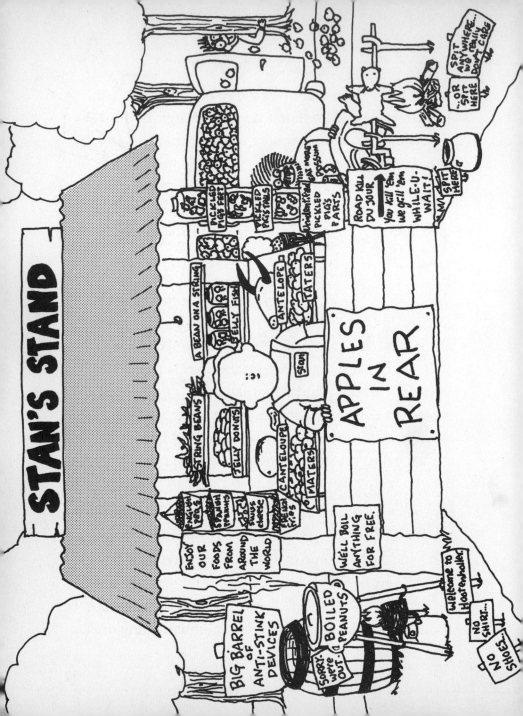

We knew Stan was in for a day of embarrassment if we didn't do something about his sign. Kids were sure to poke fun at him, saying things like...

We squatted behind a big oak while Uncle Stinky painted a new sign. As he finished, he slapped his brush down and said, "Here's where your compact size, quickness, and agility come in handy, my brave little sidekick." Then he handed me the sign and gave me a wink.

While Stan was turned around counting his exotic gourds, I put the new sign over his embarrassing one.

""Hooooooo-wheeee! Zack changed that sign quicker 'n a flash. And he threw in some fancy flips just fer the fun of it! Stan did not know that his sign had been changed until the end of the day. And he never found out who did it, either. Which was fine with us, 'cause we're uncomfortable with folks thankin' us and praisin' us anyway. We're happy just knowin' that Stan went through an entire day without sufferin' any embarrassment!

"(By the way, I thought you might wanna know that every Friday, Stan's Stand features a stew o' stuff they haven't sold. Ya wanna guess who makes the stew? Their other son, Stu. Ya wanna know who counts the money? Their daughter, Penny.)"

who cweans da potty?

John.

Close to suppertime, we headed back through town toward home. As we passed Wendell's Eggs-N-Things, Uncle Stinky stopped dead in his tracks.

"We got ourselves a CODE RED, little buddy!"

I looked and saw Mrs. Filbert loaded down with a couple of sackloads of doorknobs and a weed whacker wedged under her left armpit. She seemed to be totally unaware of what was painfully obvious to us: with each step she took, her pants were slowly slipping down.

We began calculating our options:

"Mrs. Filbert lives all the way over on Shiney Moon Avenue, right?"

"Right, little buddy. And taking into account the rate of descent of her polyesters..."

"I estimate that just about the time
she turns onto Deep Valley Road..."

"...the entire town'll be gettin' a gander
at her underpanties...or somethin' worse!"

"We can't let that happen, Unk. Here's where
your height, strength, and deep sense of
compassion come in handy. Mrs. Filbert's pants need pulling up and..."

"Say no more, little buddy."

Ol' Stinky knew that if Mrs.
Filbert were going to make it all
the way home, her pants would
need to be pulled up a little fur-
ther than normal. In fact, he
knew that if he were going to
keep all of Hootenholler
from seeing what they
ought not see, he had to
give her a bit of a wedgie.

UPSIE DAISEY.

CORN FL

"I was more than happy to help Mrs. Filbert like I did. She was so surprised that anyone could be so thoughtful.

"In all of the excitement and in her desire to express her appreciation, she twirled around, forgettin' all about them sacks o' doorknobs. As she spun to see her hero, her weed whacker whacked Herman Hornblower, who was just comin' out of the Corn Flake Café.

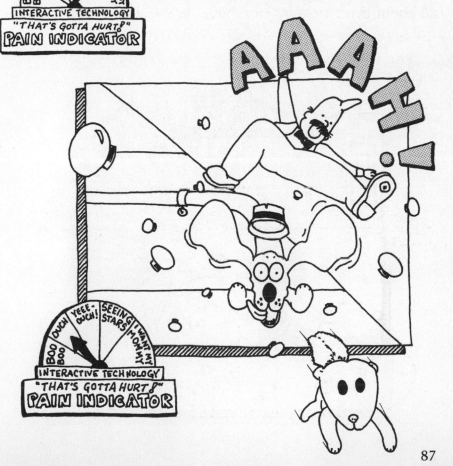

"Mr. Hornblower was busy rubbin' the bulgin' bump on his head when Lester came chasin' that same ol' squirrel.

"Ol' Lester slipped on Mrs. Filbert's doorknobs, plowed into Mr. Hornblower, and took his legs right out from under him.

"As he went down, Mr. Hornblower took Mrs. Filbert's legs out from under *her*.

"She flew up in the air a few dozen feet...

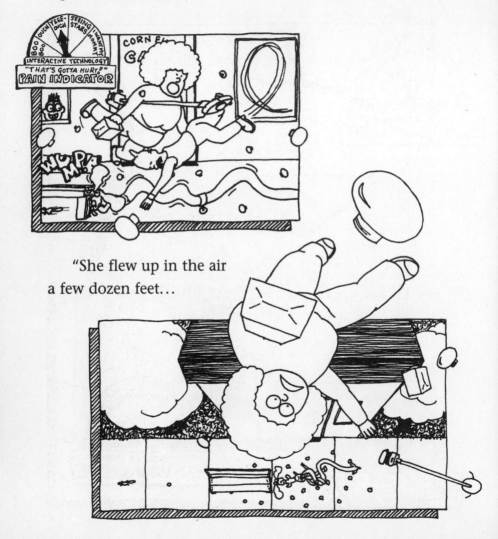

"Luckily Mr. Hornblower broke her fall or it could have been a bad situation.

"I know Mrs. Filbert wanted to thank me for what I did, but I don't need a lot of praise like some people do, so I quietly slipped away. Just the pleasure of knowing that no one was embarrassed was enough reward for me. Lester was blushing a little as he wobbled back into Belinda's Baloney Boutique...but at least no one saw what no one should see of Mrs. Filbert's."

As the sun set over Hooten-holler, Uncle Stinky felt a great happiness in his heart knowing that an entire day had passed and not one single person suffered any real embarrassment.